Lesley Ely lives in an old stable, loves sunflowers and often sees small angels in school playgrounds. She thinks big angels are harder to spot because they have better disguises! Lesley Ely has also written *Looking After Louis,* winner of the NASEN Special Needs Award, for Frances Lincoln.

Angels were one of **Polly Dunbar**'s favourite things to draw when she was younger. Once she made an angel collage out of leaves and twigs on tissue paper. It had a pressed daisy chain for a halo and gingko leaves for wings. It still hangs on the wall in a golden frame.
Polly has also illustrated *Looking After Louis* by Lesley Ely, and *Bubble Trouble* and *Down The Back of the Chair* by Margaret Mahy for Frances Lincoln.

For Maia and Gina – L.E.
For Barbara – P.D.

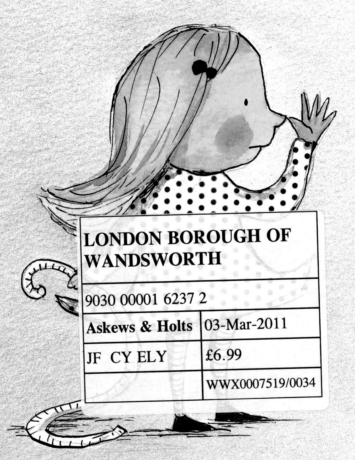

Measuring Angels copyright © Frances Lincoln Limited 2008
Text copyright © Lesley Ely 2008
Illustration copyright © Polly Dunbar 2008

The right of Lesley Ely to be identified as the Author and of Polly Dunbar to be identified as the Illustrator of this work
has been asserted by them in accordance with the Copyright, Designs and Patents Act, 1988.

First published in Great Britain and in the USA in 2008 by Frances Lincoln Children's Books,
4 Torriano Mews, Torriano Avenue, London NW5 2RZ
www.franceslincoln.com

First paperback published in Great Britain in 2011

ISBN: 978-1-84780-048-0

Printed in Singapore by Tien Wah Press (Pte) Ltd, in September 2010

1 3 5 7 9 8 6 4 2

Measuring Angels

Angels

Lesley Ely ★ Polly Dunbar

F

FRANCES LINCOLN
CHILDREN'S BOOKS

My friend Gabriel believes in angels. But he doesn't know where we'd ever find one.

   "You'll never find a real one," said Sophie. "Angels are IMAGINARY!"

So we asked Miss Miles, but she wasn't much help.

Gabriel said, "Our school is happy. Perhaps we don't need an angel."

But school wasn't happy for me.

School was horrible and it was all Sophie's fault.

   Sophie was my friend but then she stopped liking me.
I had nobody to play with at playtime because everybody
wanted to play with her.

   I saw her whisper to people when she thought
I wasn't looking. Then they looked at me.

I felt like they all hated me and I wanted to cry.

I squeezed my eyes tight shut to keep the tears in.

I stuck my tongue out and I wished I was bigger.

Gabriel found a good book
about angels. They had
wings like swans.
So we watched the sky.

One day swans flew so low over our playground

we could hear the *Whoosh! Whoosh!* of their wings.

They were powerful... and so beautiful.

But they weren't angels.

Gabriel drew an angel with curly hair like Miss Miles.
But Miss Miles isn't an angel. Angels bring good news
and Miss Miles brought bad news!

"Let's have a sunflower-growing competition!" she said.
"We've only got enough pots for one between two so we'll
have to share."

Then she gave ME a pot and she gave SOPHIE the seed
to go in it! Why did she do that? She knew me and Sophie
weren't friends!

When I put soil in the pot Sophie frowned.
She snatched the seed and shoved it hard
into the soil! I frowned but nobody noticed.

We put all our pots in a row so they were easy to measure.
I felt sure our sunflower wouldn't win. I thought Sophie would
make it feel so bad it might not grow at all.

Every day we watered our sunflowers. Sophie always grabbed the watering can before I could get it. She almost drowned our little sunflower shoot. Every time we measured the sunflowers ours was ALWAYS the weediest!

"This sunflower isn't happy," said Miss Miles. "Why don't you talk to it? Talking to plants sometimes helps them grow."

So we tried. We got close. We whispered.

"We know you're doing your best," I said.

Sophie giggled. Then she said, "You're really trying!" And we both laughed.

We talked to our plant every day after that.

It grew a little but it still looked limp and tiny.

I thought it might even die.

One day Gabriel said, "I wonder if flowers have angels?" and suddenly... I had an idea!

"Could we MAKE an angel, Miss Miles?" I asked.

"Yes," said Miss Miles.

So we did! We made a sunflower angel! Gabriel, Sophie and me! We gave her a cardboard tube body, a halo of yellow curly paper hair and wings like a golden swan! We glued paper, tissue and a whole pillow of feathers! We made our angel as tall as Miss Miles and we painted her the sunniest colours! She was glorious!

We put her next to our plant pot.

"She's taking care," whispered Sophie, "like a real angel would."

That night I dreamed our angel grew
and filled the sky. A whole field of sunflowers
turned their heads to look at her.

Our angel was waiting for us at school the next morning.
But she wasn't the way I remembered her. She seemed smaller,
ordinary, just cardboard and paper... and feathers falling off.

I looked over at our real sunflower. I expected it to be
weedy and small like before, but I was wrong! Our sunflower
was changed too! It stood straight! It stood tall! It was strong!
And it had a face like the real sun — just beautiful.

Then I saw Sophie looking at me.

Not at the sunflower... at ME.

She was smiling a HUGE smile.

It felt... like sunshine.

So I smiled back.

"No measuring today!" said Miss Miles.

"Measuring Time is cancelled!"

So we measured... nothing.

After all, it's hard to measure a smile
and nobody can measure an angel.

MORE TITLES FROM FRANCES LINCOLN CHILDREN'S BOOKS

Looking After Louis
Lesley Ely
Illustrated by Polly Dunbar

"There's a new boy at school called Louis. He's not quite like the rest of us. He often just sits there and stares at the wall. If I ask him what he's looking at he just says, 'Looking at' and carries on looking." This gentle picture book shows how – with kindness and imagination – Louis' classmates find a way to join him in his world and include Louis in theirs.

Bubble Trouble
Margaret Mahy
Illustrated by Polly Dunbar

What a terrible thing to lose a baby brother in a bubble! Follow the hilarious efforts of Mabel and the townsfolk as they work together to save Baby – and rascal rebel Abel whose pebble and sling are ready to triple trouble! Can Mabel and friends save her brother and the day?

The No-No Bird
Andrew Fusek Peters & Polly Peters
Illustrated by Jim Coplestone

No-No Bird's favourite word is No! He says No to everyone and No to everything. No he won't play with Little Mouse! No he won't climb trees with Squirrel. Then he meets Snake and learns that Snake's favourite food is No-No Bird. Can No-No Bird escape from a sticky end by changing his favourite word to Yes?

Frances Lincoln titles are available from all good bookshops.
You can also buy books and find out more about your favourite titles,
authors and illustrators on our website: www.franceslincoln.com